TEENY HOUDINI

BOOK 3:
THE GIANT PANDA PLAN

POWER!
BOOK BAGS

This Book
Belongs To: **Elijah**

www.powerbookbags.org

The TEENY HOUDINI Series

TEENY HOUDINI

BOOK 3:
THE GIANT PANDA PLAN

BY **KATRINA MOORE**   ILLUSTRATIONS BY **ZOE SI**

KATHERINE TEGEN BOOKS
An Imprint of HarperCollins Publishers

Katherine Tegen Books is an imprint of HarperCollins Publishers.

Teeny Houdini #3: The Giant Panda Plan
Text copyright © 2022 by Katrina Moore
Illustrations copyright © 2022 by Zoe Si

Library of Congress Control Number: 2021953150
ISBN 978-0-06-300466-5 (trade bdg.) — ISBN 978-0-06-300468-9 (pbk.)

Typography by Andrea Vandergrift
22 23 24 25 26   PC/LSCC   10 9 8 7 6 5 4 3 2 1
❖
First Edition

For Goo Goo,
who taught me to sew
and made my childhood magical!
—K.M.

To Isla, an excellent dog
—Z.S.

DO NOT
CLIMB

1

The Zoo!

"*ROAR! ROAR!*" I call to the lions. I stand on my tippy-toes to get as close as I can to them.

"Why won't they roar back, Mom?" I ask.

"It looks like they're sleeping," Mom says. Then she pulls me down off the fence. Now I can't see the animals! I try to climb back up. But Mom gives me her serious look and says, "Don't be *trouble*."

I am Bessie Lee. Mom calls me trouble.

Sometimes. Gramma calls me Gah Yee, my Chinese name. Bailey, my ten-year-old sister, calls me annoying. And everyone calls me teeny. Because I *am* teeny. I am the teeniest in my ribbon-dancing class. I am the teeniest in my first-grade class *and* in my family. And right now, I am the teeniest and *only* one who cannot see the lions at our first-grade field trip to the zoo.

I blink my eyes real slow. And show Mom my sweetest smile.

"Mom, can you carry me?" I ask. "Please?" I add, so she knows I am using my good manners. She picks me up. It worked. Ta-da!

"Why are you being carried like a baby?" Margo asks.

Margo is my classmate. She calls me a baby *a lot.* She also tattles on me when I am being trouble. Margo is never trouble. She always

follows the rules. Like the rule *you have to stay with your class buddy on the field trip*. Our first-grade teacher, Ms. Stoltz, made Margo my class buddy. Even though we are *not* buddies. But now my mom is *her* chaperone, too. A *chaperone* is the grown-up in charge. So Mom and I have to stay with Margo.

"I just want to see!" I say. I hug my mom tighter. Margo rolls her eyes.

"Bessie, over here!" Ella calls me over to her side of the exhibit. There are big tigers there!

Mom lets me down, and I run over. Margo struts over, too.

The tiger paces back and forth. Then it stops and stares right at us with its bright yellow eyes.

"Wow!" Ella says. "Tigers are so cool. They're my favorite!"

"I like the elephants better because they're smarter," Margo says. "You know they can show emotions like humans?"

She says a lot more things. But Ella and I stop listening. We pretend we are tigers and chase each other around Mom.

"What's your favorite animal?" Ella asks. She paws me with her hand. We laugh.

"I don't know," I say. I paw her back. Then we flop down on the ground like the sleeping lions. Some of Ella's long brown hair flies into my mouth.

"*Plegh*," I say, spitting out her hair. We laugh some more.

"Oh, girls," Mom says. "Get up, please."

Margo stands right next to my mom. She flips her blond hair over her shoulder.

I shrug my shoulders and huff. It makes me feel cool like Bailey.

"Can I have my wand, Mom?" I ask. I want to do a trick to make Margo disappear. Just for a teeny bit.

I call myself Teeny Houdini. That's because I'm magic. Just like the greatest magician of all time, Harry Houdini. I have a magic hat, a magic wand, a special magic cape, and a real bunny, Baby Rabbit. Plus, Gramma gave me a book, *Abracadabra: Magic for Kids*. It's full of magic tricks. Bailey helps me practice them if I beg her enough. I packed all my stuff in my backpack, which Mom is carrying for me, just in case. You never know when you might need magic!

"No magic at the zoo, Bessie. *Remember?*" Mom reminds me.

Oh, boo. I'm stuck with Margo.

"Did you like the gorillas?" asks Ella. She helps me up off the ground.

"Yeah!" I pretend to be a gorilla. "Ooh-ooh-ee-ee," I say, pounding my chest. "But they're not my favorite."

I don't know which animal is my favorite yet.

Ding. Ding. Ms. Stoltz rings the teacher's bell. She brings it with her everywhere.

"Attention, class! Gather around," Ms.

Stoltz calls. She waits for all the chaperones and our whole class to come near her.

Margo stands right in front of me. Now I can't see again. My friend Jae spots me and waves me over to him. He scoots over so I have a space in the front.

"Thanks!" I whisper. Jae nods and smiles.

"First graders, I want you to meet Ms. Deer. She is a zookeeper. That means she is a zoo animal expert. Her job is to take excellent care of the animals. And she is going to take us to visit someone very special . . . the newest animal here!

"Before we go on, I want you to find your partner. And find your chaperone. We're all going together to the next exhibit. And we're all going to walk. Right?"

We all nod. I cannot wait to hear what

animal we are going to meet. And Ms. Stoltz said it is new! Is it a baby? I bounce up and down.

"Okay, everyone. Are you ready to meet the baby panda?"

BABY PANDA?!

Ooh-la-laddie!

We all jump up and down.

Ms. Deer leads the way. No one walks.

We are going to meet a baby panda!

2

New Furry Friend!

The panda exhibit is surrounded by bamboo walls. There is a large grassy area with tall trees and giant rocks, a fun playground, and a hammock. There are shady spots and sunny spots, too. Everyone runs to the outdoor area. They point and shout at a giant panda that's sitting on a branch in a tree.

Except me. I keep running until I get to the indoor viewing area under the rock tunnel.

"Gramma! Daddy!" I shout.

I hug Gramma around the waist. She hugs me back and pats me on the head.

"Shh," says Daddy. He brings his index finger to his lips. "We're not supposed to be here, remember?" Daddy winks.

I am supposed to have only one chaperone on the field trip. But Mom likes us to do everything together. That's why she told Daddy and Gramma to come. Bailey would be here, too, but Mom says she can't miss school. Mom told them to camouflage so no one knows they are here. *Camouflage* means you wear the colors of the zoo to be sneaky like a ninja. Daddy's wearing a green golf shirt, khakis, and a safari hat. Gramma's wearing a brown sweater vest over her silk shirt. No one knows they are here.

"Hello, Mr. Lee. Hello, Mrs. Lee," Margo

greets them. Then she looks right at me. "You're *not* supposed to run, Bessie."

I bet she's going to tattle on me. But Mom comes over and says, "Thanks for catching up to Bessie, Margo. You're such a good partner."

Margo smiles.

Gramma taps my shoulder. She points to the panda bear den.

"Where's the baby panda?" I ask.

I press my hands and face against the glass. Ooh-la-laddie!

In the back corner of the den, I spy the baby panda! It's sitting like a teddy bear. It is white and black and the cutest animal I ever saw. Except for Baby Rabbit. But the baby panda is even fluffier than Baby Rabbit.

Slup. Slup. Slup. The baby panda licks something orange and gooey off a big red ball.

"What's it eating?" Margo asks.

"Sweet potato," Ms. Deer, the zookeeper, says.

Our whole class is around us now. Ms. Deer tells us more about the baby panda. She points to a sign with his name on it, Xiao Qi Ji. I stay pressed against the glass as I listen.

"This is *Shiau Chi Ji*, our newest panda," the zookeeper continues. "He's only five months old. He loves sweet potatoes. Mostly, though, he still drinks his mom's milk. His mom is the panda you saw up in the tree in the outdoor enclosure. Since Xiao is so young, he still spends most of his time in the den. His name translates as 'little miracle' in English."

The zookeeper keeps talking, but I hear only a little bit of what she says.

I am mesmerized by Xiao! *Mesmerized* means you cannot look away because your new furry friend is so cute that you get tingly in the knees.

"You are a little miracle," I whisper to Xiao.

Slup. Slup. Sl— The baby panda looks up. Sweet potato is slushed all over his fuzzy little face.

"He's moving!" my friend Gorkem shouts.

Now everyone crowds around the glass

that separates us from the baby panda. I am squished against the glass. At least I'm still in the front.

The baby panda crawls toward us.

"He's heading right for Bessie!" Whitney's eyes are the largest of our class.

My heart goes *thump-thump-thump* as he comes closer. All my classmates scoot closer to me to be near the baby panda. But I do not take my eyes off him. Everything else becomes blurry. Like when there's lots of stuff on the pantry shelf but you have superfocus and find the cheesy doodles hidden in the corner. I love cheesy doodles! But right now, I think I love baby Xiao even more.

Xiao stands up on his back legs. He lifts his fluffy front paws.

"Awww!" we all say.

Then he takes one paw and presses it where my hand is. If the glass was not here, we would be holding hands. I stand very still. My smile is so big it touches my eyes. My heart goes *thud-thud-thud.* Xiao squeals. He's looking right at me.

Two of my classmates, Brayden and Chris, scoot closer to me.

"Lucky Bessie!" Brayden says. "The panda likes her."

"More like loves her!" Chris says.

"I love you, too," I whisper to Xiao. He squeals again.

"Maybe he's squealing because he's sad," Margo says.

"Actually, regular loud squeals are signs of a healthy cub!" the zookeeper says. "He's trying to play with her. How sweet! Speaking of sweet . . . ," Ms. Deer continues.

But I cannot focus on what she is saying. Xiao now puts his other paw where my other hand is. He is squealing like crazy. His little black nose is pressed against the glass. He is trying to hug me.

I wish I could hug him, too! We could eat sweet potatoes together. And I could give him bamboo from Gramma's garden. He could eat all the bamboo he wants. I would eat cheesy doodles instead. Xiao would love to play with Baby Rabbit, too.

The glass between me and Xiao is all fogged up. Because he keeps squealing and breathing with his cute little nose smushed up against it. I make my side fog, too. Then I trace a heart with my finger on the glass. I made a heart around his head. I love the baby panda.

"There's a really large threat to pandas," Ms. Deer says.

I quickly turn around. *Threat* means something really bad will happen. Like when

I make a mess in Bailey's room and she threatens to tell Mom and Daddy if I don't clean it all up. But this threat seems much worse. Because Ms. Deer's voice is slow and serious.

I stand very still. And do not blink. And I make my ears very big, too.

"There are fewer than nineteen hundred giant pandas living in the wild. The largest threat to them is habitat destruction. That means people are cutting down the forests where they live."

"Who is destroying their homes?" I ask. "I will stop them!"

"Well," Ms. Deer sighs. "We all are. All people. Pandas used to live in lowland areas. But because people wanted to farm and build houses and shops, they cleared the forests— the pandas' homes. Now the pandas are isolated, or far away, from each other. They

can't find each other and make new panda families. So there are fewer and fewer pandas. At one point, they were endangered. Now they are vulnerable. Things are better, but they still need our help. They are still in danger of losing their homes and not being able to reproduce, or make enough baby pandas to keep pandas around for a long time."

My chest begins to get all tight. My eyes start to sting.

Xiao chirps behind me. I feel his breath on my back through the glass.

He paws the glass. I turn around and lean my forehead against the glass. I press my hand to his paw.

"I will help you, baby Xiao. I promise," I whisper.

It will take a miracle to help him.

Or maybe . . . some magic.

Good thing I am Teeny Houdini!

3

A Magical Plan!

After the panda exhibit, I race to Ms. Stoltz. I need a plan to save baby Xiao and the giant pandas. What is my plan? *I do not know.* But it will be magical! I cannot wait to tell Ms. Stoltz.

I tug-tug-tug the back of her sweater. Except she is not paying attention to me.

"Hurry along, friends," Ms. Stoltz calls to us all. She zips away from me to the front of the group. "We have to stick to our schedule! It's time for our picnic. Then we'll see some more animals."

I will have to wait to make a magical plan! *Waiting is the worst!*

Mom finds a shady spot to set up our picnic. "What about this spot, girls?"

"It's great, Mrs. Lee," Margo answers.

Mom doesn't wait for me to respond. She lays out the picnic blanket. Margo sits down like a proper princess.

"It's too far from Ms. Stoltz." I pout. I stomp my foot.

"*Bessie Lee,*" Mom scolds, "you know better than to act like that. Let Ms. Stoltz enjoy her lunch. We'll enjoy ours, too. Why don't you see what Gramma packed us?"

"Fine," I huff. Yummy food helps me think,

anyway. I plop onto the blanket. I peek into the cooler that Gramma gave Mom before she and Daddy left the zoo.

Ooh-la-laddie! Gramma packed me an egg-and-ham sandwich, oranges, and two teeny lychee jelly cups. *Yum!* I slurp down the lychee jelly cups first.

Now I am ready to think of a plan to save baby Xiao. I dig into my backpack and pull out my magic wand. If I tap-tap-tap my wand to my forehead, maybe an idea will appear. I say my extra fancy magic word that makes magic appear, "Abracadabra-poof!"

"Bessie," Mom says slowly. She makes her eyes big and her mouth tiny. That means I have to put my wand away. "Finish eating your lunch, like Margo. Look how good she is!" She pats Margo's knee.

Margo grins. Then she takes a dainty bite out of her heart-shaped sandwich with cucumbers and cream cheese. I chomp into my sandwich. It's sweet and eggy. Gramma makes the best sandwiches.

"Mrs. Lee, do you know what I learned about the elephants today?" Margo asks.

"Please, tell me," Mom replies. She bites into the pineapple bun that Gramma packed for her.

"Well, you saw how they were playing with that tire swing?"

Mom turns to Margo and nods. She gives her all her attention.

"I read on the sign that their trunks are so strong . . . ," Margo continues. She says a lot more stuff, but I stop listening.

I finish my lunch . . . mostly. Then I pull my wand out, again, and also my magician's hat. This will help me think of a magical plan! How can I help the baby panda? I need to focus.

Ooh! A peacock walks by us. It is bright

blue with long green feathers and so, so, so fancy! Mom and Margo are too busy talking to notice. But not me!

I jump up to greet the peacock. "Hi, birdy! I'm Teeny Houdini!"

The peacock just looks at me. Then it keeps walking. I follow it.

Where is it going?

We walk up and down, around all the picnic blankets. Next, we cross under a fence. I have to crawl only a little bit to get through.

The sun shines on the peacock's back and makes it shimmer. The peacock's tail trails behind it like a royal cape. I wish I'd grabbed my magician's cape! But I walk like I am royal, anyway—just like the peacock!

Finally, the peacock stops and turns around. It fans out its feathers like a giant green, gold, and blue polka-dot rainbow. It is putting on a show! Ooh-la-laddie!

But then it comes toward me and calls, "CAH! CAH! CAH!"

It pokes its beak near my face.

AHHH! I run, and run, and run, as fast as my teeny legs will let me. I do not stop until I smack into Ms. Stoltz's sweater.

"Oh, Bessie," Ms. Stoltz sighs. "We were looking all over for you." She pushes her glasses up her nose.

"Bessie Lee!" Mom yells. She scoots through the group to get to me. "You had me worried to death!"

"I almost did die, Mom!" I explain. "The peacock almost ate me! But good thing I am superfast and got away."

"You shouldn't wander off," Mom scolds. She makes her lips tiny like she is mad.

I give Mom a supersqueeze. "It's okay, Mom. I am smarter than the peacock." She sighs and hugs me back.

"What peacock?" Ms. Stoltz asks. She looks around.

"The one putting on the show!" I say. "I had to follow it. I *had to*. It was calling all my attention." *That's it!* I tap-tap-tap my magician's hat with my wand. I know my magical plan now! I jump up and down.

"Ms. Stoltz! Ms. Stoltz!" I yell.

"Yes, Bessie," she answers. She checks our names off her clipboard to make sure we are all still here.

"Our class should save the giant pandas! Remember what zoo lady said? They need our help," I say, using my big-kid voice, like Bailey does. I stand supertall. I speak loudly. But slowly and calmy, too.

"They do need our help," Ms. Stoltz agrees. "I think that's an excellent idea for our class to help the pandas. How should we do that?"

"We can put on a fun show! Like the peacock! Except it's the panda show! And it can have magic in it!" I suggest. I bounce-bounce-bounce in place.

Everyone starts talking at once about their ideas for the show.

Ms. Stoltz pulls the bell out of her sweater pocket.

Ding. Ding. Ding.

"Let's take turns sharing our ideas on how to save the pandas. We heard Bessie's plan to put on a panda show and include magic. What are some other suggestions?"

"I like Bessie's plan!" Ella says.

"Me too," Jae agrees.

"I have a better one," Margo smirks. "Why don't we give a PowerPoint presentation? We can invite the whole community."

Whitney nods. "Ooh, I like that, Margo!"

Brayden raises his hand. He says, "What if we make a giant panda habitat?"

"Yea!" Chris and Gorkem say at the same time.

"Well, friends," Ms. Stoltz replies, "you all have some wonderful suggestions." She thinks for a moment.

"Okay, let's put on a panda showcase before we leave for spring break. We'll put up signs and invite the entire community. Our showcase will try to fundraise, or collect money donations, to help pandas. That gives us a few days to put together the plan we want to use. I'll then choose the best one.

"Why don't you split up into teams? Bessie, Margo, and Brayden will be the team leaders. Then each team can present their plan to me on Thursday, and we'll have the panda showcase on Friday!"

"Yes!" we all agree. Even the monkeys and birds behind us cheer.

Ella and Jae zoom over to me.

"We're on your team, Bessie!" Ella says. Jae nods along.

"Wahoo!" I sing. Then I toss my magician's hat into the air.

It's time to plan the panda show!

4

A Tricky Knot!

When we get home from the zoo, I plan to get right to work. I need to practice for the panda show! But first I flop onto my bed. Baby Rabbit hops onto my belly. She sniffs me all over. It tickles. I giggle.

"Hi, Baby Rabbit!" I say, and then I kiss her wet nose. She sniffs my face. Maybe she smells baby Xiao and the other zoo animals on me. Or maybe she smells my lunch.

"Are you hungry, girl?" I ask. Her ears stick straight up. She is! I dig into my secret stash of snacks under my bed. I plop some blueberries onto the bed for Baby Rabbit. I choose cheesy doodles for myself.

Baby Rabbit and I eat, and eat, and eat. And we take a little snooze.

After a teeny nap, I am ready to practice for the panda show! Ella is going to dress like a panda bear. Jae is going to write a script for us to act out. My part of the panda show is to wow the crowd with magic! Then everyone will want to give money to help the pandas. Ms. Deer said the money donated to the zoo helps teams to study pandas. That way they know how to help them.

I get out my notebook and draw baby Xiao. Baby Rabbit climbs on my head while I work.

"Isn't he sweet, Baby Rabbit?" I ask. She leans over my face to get a better look. I remember my promise to the baby panda. *I will help you, baby Xiao.*

Next, I pull out my *Abracadabra: Magic for Kids* book. This has all the magic tricks I've done in it. Plus more that I have to learn. What trick should I perform for the panda show? I flip. And flip. And flip through the book.

I finally find the perfect page! "'THE BIG BEAR K-NOT,'" I read. On the page is a thick rope tied into a bear-looking knot. A KNOT! It is a silent *k* . . . tricky, tricky! I will have to remember to tell Ms. Stoltz how I used my magician's eye to figure out the tricky word. She will be so proud. She will probably say, *You are so smart, Bessie!* And I will say, *I know!*

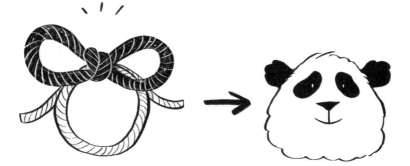

The next picture on the page shows a magician holding the rope. The bear knot is gone. It has vanished. But how?!

I try to read the words on the page. But the words are too tricky. I pop out of bed. Bailey can help me!

I dash down the hall to Bailey's room. Her door is wide open. Normally, she locks it. But she forgot today!

"Bailey?" I skip into her room. I run my hand along her ballet barre. Then I spy something special in her closet. One of her costumes from her dance recital. It is black and white like a panda, and fuzzy ALL OVER. Ooh-la-laddie! This is *perfect* for our panda show.

I tug the costume down off the hanger. I try to be careful to show respect. But I have to jump-jump-jump to reach the costume. It makes me knock down a few other things in her closet. By accident.

But look at me! I twirl around in front of Bailey's mirror. I fix my hair so my ponytails

are extra fluffy—like panda ears! This is perfect. Now I just have to ask Bailey for permission to wear her costume. *Permission* is when you check that what you did is okay. It shows you have good manners. Where is Bailey?

Baby Rabbit follows me as we hop around the house. We are using our magician's eyes to look for Bailey. She is very good at disappearing from me. But good thing I am a great magician—just like Harry Houdini.

In Mom and Daddy's room, I do not find Bailey. We spy Daddy on the phone. I try to show him my panda costume. But he holds up a finger. And twirls his desk chair away from me. *Boo.* It must be a serious lawyer business call. I know because I see two coffee mugs on his desk.

In the bathroom, I do not spy Bailey. I spy Mom taking a shower. I try to get in to show her my panda costume. But she says, "Bessie, give me some privacy, please!" So I get out of the shower. I am only a little bit wet.

In the kitchen, I do not spy Bailey. Or Gramma. But I do smell Gramma's chicken and winter melon soup. *Yum!* I lift the lid. It needs more color. I pull some crayons that I have tucked in my sock *just in case*. Like *just in case* I want to turn Gramma's soup rainbow colors! I unwrap red, orange, yellow, green, blue, purple, and pink crayons. Then I plop them into the soup. I cover the lid. Then I tap one, two, three times

and say, "Abracadabra-poof!" When I open the lid, the soup is rainbow colors. Hooray!

But I still need to find Bailey to help me with the Big Bear Knot trick. And to ask permission for the costume I am wearing.

I spy with my magician's eye that Gramma is in the garden outside! I scoop my magician's assistant, Baby Rabbit, into my arms and run into the backyard.

Gramma is kneeling. She's wearing gloves and digging into her garden beds. Little tomato plants in green cups sit beside her. She is covered in dirt.

"Hi, Gramma!" I plop next to her. Now I am covered in dirt, too.

Baby Rabbit knocks over one of the tomato plants and nibbles the leaves.

"Ay yah!" Gramma shouts. She shoos Baby Rabbit away from her plant. Baby Rabbit finds clover in the yard to munch on instead.

Gramma takes her hands out of the gloves. She cups my cheeks. And she squeezes. "Gah Yee," Gramma says softly. She smiles.

It makes me warm all over. Gramma talks to me in Chinese and points to different things in her garden. I do not understand what she's saying. But I like listening, anyway. I hand her a tomato plant. When she is done talking, I ask her, "Do we have rope?" I point to the picture in my magic book.

"Oh!" Gramma says. She does not understand what I say, but she knows what I want. She points to the other side of the garden bed. There are pepper plants and tall vines tied to a stick with rope. Rope! There's extra rope lying on the grass.

"Thank you, Gramma!" I cheer. I run over to the rope. It is not as thick as the rope in the picture, but I can fix that!

I cut and glue the rope together. This makes a thicker rope like in the magic book. Then I paint it black and white like a panda. I do it all outside to be responsible. Because it is a teeny bit messy.

When Bailey finally comes home, she spies me in the backyard. She is shocked that I look so fancy. Perfect timing! Now she can help me learn the Big Bear Knot trick!

5

Panda Problems

Bailey shouts at me for a super-duper long time.

I stand still and make my ears very big. I listen. But Baby Rabbit hides behind my feet. She does not like shouting.

Finally, I cut in. "I am sorry, Bailey! I was trying to ask you for permission. I am doing it to save the baby pandas. Please, can I wear it? And, please, can you help me practice?" I smile big. I blink my eyes real slow. This is my I-am-trying-to-be-sweet face. Bailey opens her mouth to scream some more.

"Look!" I interrupt so she won't get mad. I show her my drawing of baby Xiao.

She stares at my drawing for a billion breaths. Finally, she sighs. "Okay, FINE! I'll help you. And I guess you can wear this, too." Bailey tugs the tutu of her ballet costume I am wearing.

I squeal. And squeeze her tight. She rolls her eyes.

"All right, Teeny Houdini. What's the trick?" Bailey asks.

I show her the page with the BIG BEAR KNOT! Bailey reads the words from the book. And I practice the hand movements. Sometimes I add in fancy twirls and jumps. For fun.

Bailey puts her head in her hands. She reads the words slower. Louder. I get a little tangled in the rope. Then I get a lot tangled. Finally, she holds my hands and shows me what the instructions say.

After a trillion-bajillion hours, I do the trick right *one time*! Bailey says now I will not need help from her for forever. She is the best big sister!

The next day at school, Ella, Jae, and I huddle together in gym class. Our gym teacher, Ms. Wolff, blows her whistle. She tells us it is free play day! There are jump ropes, Frisbees, and a tub of balls. Then she starts throwing big bouncy balls around the gym. Ella, Jae, and I move out of the way. We lean our heads together.

"Did you find a trick to do?" Ella asks me. We have to whisper. We cannot let the other teams hear our plan.

"I did it!" I whisper-yell. I tell them all about the Big Bear Knot trick. I also share how I painted the rope black and white like a panda bear.

"That's perfect!" Ella says. Jae nods and smiles.

Ella continues, "My *papá* found some black-and-white fabric for the panda bear costume. Your grandma can help me sew it, right?" She wrinkles her eyebrows. That's what Ella does when she wants someone to say yes. But does not know if they will.

"Yes," I say. "Gramma's the best sewer! Remember how she made my magic cape?"

"Right!" Ella replies. "Then we just need to write the script. Jae, did you do your part?"

Jae's smile grows bigger. Jae cups his hands around his mouth. He whispers, "I checked out a ton of books about pandas from the library. We can take notes from them to write the script."

He cracks his knuckles. He's showing us he means business.

Business is important stuff you have to do. Like making the best plan to present to Ms.

Stoltz for the panda showcase. So you can wow the crowd. And get them to care about the pandas. *Business* is when you have to save baby Xiao.

Margo waltzes over to us. She's bouncing a green ball. It matches her green sweater-dress and sparkly green bow. Whitney comes up behind her. Her rainbow hair beads *jingle-jingle-jingle* as she bounces two balls at once.

"What are you all whispering about?" Margo asks.

"Ooh, I want to know!" Whitney says.

"We can't tell you," Ella says. She winks at Whitney.

Whitney gasps. "I know! You're talking about your plan for the panda showcase. Guess what we're doing?"

"Nothing!" Margo interrupts. She scrunches her mouth and eyebrows at Whitney. "All you need to know . . . is that it's well planned. It's fancy. And it uses really cool technology. Better than what Mr. C. taught us." Mr. C. is our computer teacher.

I gulp. Maybe our plan will not be the best after all.

Whitney pretends to double-zip her lips with her hands. The two balls bounce away.

One bounces into Brayden's back.

"Hey!" Brayden says. He turns around to see who hit him.

"Oopsie," Whitney says. "It was an accident."

Brayden laughs. We all do, too.

"Hey, Whitney," Brayden says, stretching his hand with the ball in it back behind him. A big smile spreads across his face. "Take this!" He tosses the ball back toward Whitney's legs.

"DODGEBALL!" Chris calls when he sees what's going on.

Whitney jumps to the side. "Too slow," she says. She runs after the bouncing ball.

Bounce-bounce-bounce. Catch! Whitney grabs the ball. She chucks it back at Brayden.

"He's out!" Ms. Wolff calls from across the gym. She comes over to make sure everyone is playing fair. Like when someone gets tagged out and they have to sit down.

"Drats!" Brayden grumbles as he sits.

"Let's keep it going," Ms. Wolff says. She tosses the ball back to Whitney.

Everyone cheers. Except me.

I do like dodgeball. I am teeny and fast. The ball misses me a lot. But I cannot focus on dodgeball right now. Because Margo said her plan is fancy. And full of technology.

Maybe it is better than our plan.

Do Brayden, Chris, and Gorkem have a fancy plan, too?

I go and sit down next to Brayden. Even though I am not out of the game. I need to know more about their plan! I scoot-scoot-scoot closer to him.

The dodgeball game is too loud. I yell, "What is your team presenting for the panda showcase?" I hope Brayden says their plan is not so good.

"Our plan is epic!" he replies.

"Chris's mom is an artist. She has all this stuff that we can use. We're making a HUGE panda habitat. IT. IS. EPIC," he repeats.

I have an invisible fuzz ball in my throat. It makes it feel scratchy. I try to swallow. *Epic* means the coolest, bestest in the world. Like it will definitely be the best plan of all.

I need to grab Ella and Jae. I pop up to find them when—

WHAM!

Phoooot! Ms. Wolff blows her whistle. She walks over to me and hovers over my face.

"Uh-oh, Bessie's down," Ms. Wolff says to the class.

"Are you okay?" She helps me sit back up.

"There's a big problem," I say. My tummy is sore where the ball hit me. But that is not the problem. I make my most serious face.

"What is it?" Ms. Wolff asks. She looks worried.

I turn to Ella and Jae. Their eyes are big. They stare at me. They wait for what I will say next.

I look right at them and say, "We have a panda problem."

6

Practice Makes Perfect

After school, Ella and Jae come over to my house. I tell about them Brayden, Gorkem, and Chris's epic habitat plan. And I remind them about Margo and Whitney's fancy plan, too.

I fling open the front door. Ella and Jae follow behind me.

"'Baby pandas are born blind,'" says Jae. He reads as he walks. "'They are pink, hairless, and the size of a stick of butter as newborns—'"

"We need our plan to get chosen!" I interrupt.

"Why?" Jae asks.

"Because our plan is the best!" I remind him.

"Yeah!" Ella agrees.

Jae nods slowly.

"What will we do?" I ask, throwing my backpack on the kitchen floor. I pull out my magician's cape and put it on. Wearing my cape always gives me magical ideas. That is just what we need right now. But also, food!

Gramma picks up my backpack and hangs it on the back of my chair. Then she sets out snack plates. She puts a big bowl of green grapes on the table for us.

"Thank you, Gramma!" I say, plopping a grape into my mouth.

"Thank you," Ella and Jae say together.

Gramma nods and smiles. She squeezes my shoulders, then walks away.

"My *mamãe* packed me an after-school snack, too," Ella says. She pulls a container out of her lunch box. "Can I heat it up?"

"Of course!" I reply. I show her where the microwave is. I jump up to reach the buttons for her.

As Ella's snack is heating up, I show Ella and Jae the Big Bear Knot trick. I do not wear my hat or make glitter fly out, though. I will save that for the real show.

"That's amazing!" Ella cheers.

"Bravo!" Jae says. He claps. "The knot looks like a panda bear. Then it disappears! Smart, Bessie!"

He pulls out some paper from his backpack. He scribbles.

"What are you doing?" I ask.

He doesn't respond. His head is buried in his writing. Then he pulls book, after book, after book from his backpack. They all have panda bears on them.

"He's taking notes," Ella says. I nod.

"How'd you do the trick so good?" Ella asks.

"I practiced for a million-gazillion hours!" I tell her. *Ooh!* That's it!

"We just have to practice, practice, practice our show," I say. "Practice makes perfect."

"Yeah!" Ella agrees. Jae does not respond.

He is buried in his books. He looks up and says, "Did you know pandas can only breed once a year? No wonder it's hard to repopulate."

Ella and I did not know. It is a good thing we have Jae on our team!

Beep-beep-beep. "Your snack!" I cheer. I run to the microwave to help Ella. Because Mom always says we should be good hosts. I think that means when your friends come to your house, you give them food until they complain they are too full.

Gramma helps me because the food is hot. I follow her to the table. I sniff the steam. Ella's snack smells like Gramma's beef soup. And also like spaghetti sauce.

I lean over Ella as she stirs it. I stick my tongue out like a doggie. Baby Rabbit must smell the yummy food, too. She hops into the kitchen and jumps onto my lap.

Ella pulls crispy potato sticks out of her lunch box. She sprinkles them over her creamy,

beefy rice snack. And mixes it all together.
She sees me staring.
And drooling.

Ella giggles. "It's *estrogonofe de carne*," she
says. "My *mamãe* makes it all the time." *Estrogonofe de carne* is the best-smelling beef and
cream over rice with potato chip sticks I have
ever smelled in my life.

"Do you want some?" Ella asks.

Ella scoops half of her snack onto my plate.
I gobble it up. It is as yummy as it smells. But

I save a teeny bit for Baby Rabbit. And a bite for Gramma, too.

Ella offers some to Jae, too. But he is still busy scribbling. And reading. And spreading books all over the place. He reads some more out loud.

"'Pandas are mostly solitary animals. They like to be alone.'"

While Jae does his research, Ella and I give Gramma the black-and-white fabric. I show Gramma my drawing of baby Xiao.

"Can you sew this for us Gramma?" I ask. I point to her sewing machine.

Gramma looks at my drawing. She looks over at Jae's books on the kitchen table, too.

"Oh, *hoong mow*," Gramma says. *Hoong mow* is *panda bear* in Chinese! Because Gramma points to a panda bear photograph from one of the books.

"Yes, Gramma," I say. I bounce up and down.

Gramma nods. She takes the fabric from Ella and gets to work. Gramma's sewing is magic!

Now Ella and I work on the script. But we are not so good at writing yet. Because we are learning four-letter words in school.

Good thing Bailey is the best big sister ever! When I ask her to pretty-please-with-sparkles-and-fish-gummy-candies-on-top write our script for us, she says, "You are so weird, Bessie." But she helps us, anyway.

Ella and I are codirectors. That means Ella and I can tell Bailey exactly what to write.

Our show needs to better than Margo and Whitney's plan. Better than Brayden, Chris, and Gorkem's plan, too. We need to make our plan the best!

Bailey puts her head down in her hand. She huffs superloud. I copy her. And Ella copies me. *Huff. Huff. Huff.* This makes Bailey huff some more.

"STOP!" Bailey shouts. Ella and I freeze like statues. Baby Rabbit does, too.

"Isn't this supposed to be about pandas?" Bailey asks. "Why don't you start with what you know about pandas?"

"Pandas are cute!" I say.

"They are adorable!" Ella adds.

"Baby Xiao is my forever friend," I say as my heart *thump-thump-thumps*. "He needs our help."

"Okaaaay," Bailey says. "But how are you going to convince people to help the pandas if you don't have any facts?"

"Facts?" Ella and I repeat together. My jaw drops open. FACTS? I turn to Ella. She turns to me. We do not know panda facts.

"I have facts!" Jae calls from the kitchen. He runs over. He's holding a stack of papers as thick as a book. "I have lots of panda facts." Jae's smile spreads to his eyes.

Gramma comes over, too.

"Hoong mow," Gramma says. She holds up the panda costume she sewed.

It. Is. PERFECT.

I jump up and down. Glitter flies out of my magic cape and sprinkles down over us.

Our panda show is going to be the best!

Magic or . . .

Ding. Ding. Ms. Stoltz rings her teacher bell. It is Thursday. Today we will show her our plans. And the team with the best plan will present at the panda showcase tomorrow!

"Time to go, friends! Let's clean up our supplies. We're going to hang up posters around the school neighborhood. This will give folks plenty of time to learn about our panda showcase. When we return, each team can present to me. And then I'll choose the winning plan," Ms. Stoltz says.

"The best plan will be chosen. Right, Ms. Stoltz?" Margo asks.

"We'll see," Ms. Stoltz replies.

Everyone runs around with crayons and markers. I push the cap on my marker real tight. I don't want it to dry out like last time. Then I close my school box. And jump in line. Ella saved me a spot behind her.

"Look at my poster!" I say. I show her the swirly letters I made so the poster is extra special.

"That's spelled wrong," Margo cuts in. She stands behind me. "Help is spelled *h-e-l-p*. See?" She shows us her poster.

Margo points to the word *help*. "See?" she

repeats. "I also put *all* the information Ms. Stoltz told us to on it. Isn't it great?"

It is great. But I do not say that to Margo. Because she is my showcase enemy right now. Her poster *is* the greatest of all time. But I cannot let her know.

"It's okay," I lie. Then I turn tomato red. Mom always tells me it is not nice to lie!

I walk closer behind Ella so Margo does not see my face.

Ms. Stoltz reminds us to stay in line and all together. When we reach the first tree, she asks, "Whose poster should we put up here?" She holds up a big roll of tape.

"How about mine?" Margo suggests. She shows her poster to Ms. Stoltz.

"Wow, Margo! That's fantastic! You put all the information we need on it. Great job," Ms. Stoltz says. She tapes Margo's poster to the tree.

We keep walking. And taping poster. After poster. After poster.

"That's my house!" Gorkem calls, pointing to a pretty stone house with a lady standing in front of it. "Hi, Mom!"

"Hello, Ms. Kaya!" Ms. Stoltz calls.

Gorkem's mom waves to us. She lets us tape two posters to the trees in front of her house.

Finally, Ms. Stoltz tapes my poster to a tree at the end of the street. I look around. There are no houses near here. Maybe she did not want anyone to see my poster. Because it is not as great as Margo's. I shrink my head down. I am teenier now.

But on the walk back to school, I spy with

my magician's eye a pink petal on the side-walk. A cherry blossom petal! I find more. And more. And more. I feel a teeny bit better now. Soon, both my pockets are filled with pink petals. Ooh-la-laddie!

"Ms. Stoltz, Bessie's not staying in line," Margo tattles. Of course.

"Bessie, you know better than that," Ms. Stoltz turns around to say. "Stay in line, please."

I huff. "Wait until our big show," I say to Margo.

"It's so great!" Ella says. She skips. "We have a script that is so funny. And Bessie's magic trick is AMAZING!"

"Is it really magic?" Margo questions. "Or . . . is it like when you made Rufus disappear?" Rufus is our class pet hamster. I made him disappear in the fall. But then Margo found him and said it wasn't *real* magic.

"It's real magic," I reply. I turn around to look right at Margo. Then I stick my chin up so I am less teeny.

"Awesome!" Brayden says. "But ours is going to be better." He runs up next to me.

Margo raises her hand to tattle on him, too. But Ms. Stoltz does not see.

"Our habitat is the best!" Brayden

continues. "It's huge! It looks so real, too. Everyone's going to go bonkers over it."

"*Maybe*," Margo replies. "But you haven't seen our PowerPoint presentation. It's so fancy."

"We have so many cool panda facts," Whitney adds, running up behind us. "Like how a grown panda eats twenty to forty pounds of bamboo a day! And how a panda's 'thumb' is really a long wrist bone—"

Margo interrupts, "We're bringing Whitney's dad's projector and big screen. It'll look incredible outside. Like what you see in the movies. It's much better than a habitat. Or magic."

I run up to Ella.

"Did you hear that?" I whisper.

"Yeah," she says. "But what can we do?"

I don't say anything. But I imagine that I am holding my magic wand. If I had it, I would make Margo and Whitney's presentation disappear. And I would make Brayden, Chris, and Gorkem's habitat vanish, too. Then the only plan would be mine, Ella, and Jae's. And it would be the best for sure.

We cross the street back to our school. I tap-tap-tap my head. I need a real magic idea right now. *What can we do?*

I still do not know.

We head back into the classroom. Everyone is in the cubby area hanging up their jackets. But not me because I threw mine on the floor.

I am the first to sit down at my desk. Margo's desk is right next to mine. On it, there is a fancy projector. And a little thumb drive plugged in its side. A thumb drive is like a mini file folder. It holds important stuff. That's what Daddy says. Important stuff like fancy presentations. *Like Margo's.*

Will Margo and Whitney's plan be better than ours?

I turn tomato red again. But not because I lied. Because I am about to do something bad.

I pull the thumb drive out of the projector.

I make it disappear.

"Ta-da . . . ," I whisper to myself. *Now you see it. Now you don't.*

But is it magic or . . . just mean?

The projector screen turns blue. It reads
E-J-E-C-T-I-O-N E-R-R-O-R! I cannot read it.
My heart goes *thump-thump-thump.* And my
face must be red-red because it feels like fire.

Before anyone can see, I push the thumb
drive back into the projector.

Phew. That was close.

Everyone is back at their seats.

Ding. Ding.

"All right, friends," Ms. Stoltz says. She stands right in front of me. "Let's see those plans you each came up with. Margo and Whitney, you're up first. I've got your presentation ready to go."

Margo and Whitney strut to the front of the classroom. Whitney clicks the remote.

"Why you should save pandas—" Whitney begins. She clicks again. And again. And again.

Margo looks at her. "What's wrong?"

"It . . . disappeared," Whitney whispered.

Uh-oh. My eyes almost pop out.

I made their presentation disappear.

8

Mayhem

Ms. Stoltz walks over to the projector to help Whitney.

"How could your presentation just disappear? I saw it right before we left," she says. She pulls the thumb drive from the projector. Then plugs it into a computer. She leans down closer to the computer. Her star earrings dangle.

I do not go up to Ms. Stoltz to touch her earrings. Even though they are stars. And stars are magic. If I go up to Ms. Stoltz, then she will know it was me.

I made Margo and Whitney's presentation disappear.

Margo looks right at me.

I look away.

"Well," Ms. Stoltz announces to us. "I have to try to figure this out later. In the meantime, Bessie, Ella, and Jae, it's your turn. Please present your group's plan."

I gulp. I do not say anything as I follow Ella and Jae into the cubby area.

Ella pulls her panda costume out of our box. She steps into it.

"How do I look?" Ella asks. She turns around. Gramma sewed it so good.

"You look like a panda!" I cheer.

I forget about the bad thing I did a teeny bit.

I get changed into Bailey's ballet costume.

I put on my magician's cape and my magician's hat, and grab my wand, too.

"How do I look?" I ask. I hold my wand up like I am about to do a trick.

"You look like a magic panda!" Ella answers.

"What do you think, Jae?" I turn to ask.

Jae stares into the box. It's empty. But he digs and digs and digs in it, anyway.

He finally glances up. He looks like he might cry.

"Someone took our script," he says.

"Who would do that?" Ella says. She looks in the box. I do too.

Empty.

I think about the bad thing *I* did. Maybe someone else in our class did a bad thing, too. Like made our script disappear.

"Let's tell Ms. Stoltz," Ella suggests. If we tell Ms. Stoltz, then maybe she will ask about the other bad thing. Then she'll know it was me.

"No," I whisper-yell. Ella and Jae look at me all confused. "The show must go on. That's what Harry Houdini, the greatest magician of all time, would say. We will have to do it without a script. We can do it."

I lead the way to the front of the class. Inside I feel like goo with bugs crawling in my tummy. But I do not show it. Because a good performer must be confident. *Confident*

is when you act like you have your script. Even though you do not. Even though you do not remember anything you are supposed to say.

"Wow! You all look awesome," Whitney says. She wipes her wet eyes. She is sad. Because her presentation disappeared. Because of me. My heart *plop-plop-plop*s to my feet.

Ella sweats. "Welcome to the panda show!" she says.

Jae and I stand next to her. But then Jae looks at the big crowd. And scoots back behind us.

"We are going to start with a panda bear joke. Umm . . ." Ella turns to me.

I shrug my shoulders. I do not remember the joke. Or the panda facts.

The only one who does is Jae. I turn to him

and whisper-yell, "Jae . . . help us!"

Jae drops his head into his hands. He shakes his head. He is so upset.

Everyone watches us. And waits.

I bet Margo will say something like, *Excuse me, what is the joke already?* But she doesn't. She looks away. And sweats. Margo *never* sweats.

"I know. I know!" I say, jumping up and down. I remember a joke! "What does the cow say to the horse?"

Everyone just blinks.

"MOOOOOOOOOVE," I answer myself.

Everyone stops blinking.

Gorkem says, "Shouldn't you tell a panda joke?"

I do not say anything back. Because the invisible bugs in my tummy are crawling all over. And Ella looks like she will cry, too.

"Maybe it's time for the magic trick," Ms. Stoltz suggests.

"Great!" I say, trying to feel better. Magic always makes a magician feel better. I stand taller.

"Ladies and gentlemen," I begin. I set my wand down gently. I reach into the pocket of my cape. I continue, "Here is my . . ." I reach farther into the pocket. "Here is my . . ." I cannot feel it. *Where is my panda bear rope for my trick?*

"My rope is gone," I say, my lip quivering. I try super-duper-hard not to cry. I continue, "I can't do my trick without my rope." And then I fall to the floor and cry.

"Oh my," Ms. Stoltz says. "We'll figure this out, too."

She motions Ella, Jae, and me over to her desk. "Everyone else, why don't you head on out to see what Brayden, Chris, and Gorkem have planned."

Another teacher waves from the hallway. Everyone starts to follow him out. Whitney's cheeks are puffy from her crying. Margo looks tomato red. She walks with her head down. Brayden moves like a robot. His face is stiff like a robot, too. Only Chris and Gorkem look excited.

Ella, Jae, and I trudge over to Ms. Stoltz's desk. She sighs. "What happened?" she asks.

What happened?

I made Whitney and Margo's presentation disappear.

I ruined their fancy plan.

Someone stole our script. And my magic rope.

Someone ruined our magical plan.

And now it's only up to Brayden, Chris, and Gorkem to save the pandas. Only their plan can save baby Xiao.

I open my mouth to tell Ms. Stoltz everything when—

"OUR HABITAT!" Chris screams from outside.

We all rush outside to see. Even Ms. Stoltz.

The life-size panda bear habitat is knocked down. Bamboo is broken. Nothing is still standing. Everything is in clumps and heaps. It's all completely collapsed.

"IT'S RUINED!" Chris shouts again. He bursts into tears. He throws himself onto the collapsed habitat. Gorkem slumps down. And cries, too.

Brayden stomps right up . . . to me.

"YOU DID THIS! I KNOW IT! YOU

DID THIS BY MAGIC!" Brayden yells at me.

"I DID NOT!" I yell back. Because I did not. My heart starts *thump-thump-thumping* again. "Maybe it was Margo," I add.

Margo shoots back, "How can you think that? I ALWAYS follow the rules!" Then she turns around quickly and says, "Maybe it was Ella!"

"What?" Ella says, shocked.

Everyone starts shouting at once. Even the

Ding. Ding. Ding. of Ms. Stoltz's bell does not stop us.

Finally, Ms. Stoltz shouts, "ENOUGH!"

We all freeze. She takes a deep breath. Then, in her teacher voice, she says, "We all need to go inside to take a time-out."

9

The Magic
of Compromise

Mayhem is when everything is a disaster. Like you ruined someone else's plan because you were jealous. And they ruined yours. And now everything is a big, big, big mess. And no one's plan is the best. Because they are all destroyed.

Recess has started, but our class is inside. We are all in time-out. Ella, Jae, Margo, Whitney, Brayden, Gorkem, Chris, and I all sit with our heads down at our desks. We can hear the other first graders playing outside and having fun. But not us.

Ms. Stoltz told us she was disappointed. We were supposed to present a plan to save the pandas. But all we did was ruin everything. Ms. Stoltz is so disappointed that she stands in the hallway with the door cracked open.

She doesn't want to be here with us.

I want to say sorry to Whitney and Margo. But I am mad that maybe they stole my magic rope. And our script. I am mad and sad. All at once. I slump down in my chair instead.

No one else says a thing, either.

I'm watching the clock hands move slowly by. . . .

When, suddenly, Brayden walks over to

my desk. He drops my magic
rope on top.

"I'm sorry," he says. He
looks down at the floor.
His hands are clasped
together so tight that
they are white. But
Brayden's face turns red. "You're so good at
magic. I didn't want your magic trick to make
our habitat look less cool." He sniffs.

I'm shocked. But then I admit, "I was
wrong, too."

I look at Whitney and then at Margo. She's
already glaring at me. But Whitney looks sur-
prised when I say, "I'm sorry."

"I knew you messed up our presentation!"
Margo says. Then she turns away quickly.

"What about our habitat?" Chris asks.

"Who ruined that?" Everyone looks at each other. But Margo stares out the window.

No one answers.

It is silent for a million-quadrillion minutes.

Jae finally breaks the silence. His chair squeaks as he pushes it away. He stands up. He looks at each of us.

Then he says, "It doesn't matter who did it. We are all wrong. We ruined everything. We were supposed to help the pandas.

"You know, pandas are losing their homes. Because of people like us. We are arguing. But we should be focusing on the problem. Remember, the zookeeper said fewer than nineteen hundred pandas are left in their native habitat."

I take a deep breath. I think of baby Xiao. I remember why we need to help. *Who* we need to help.

"Actually, it's 1,864 pandas, to be exact," Margo corrects.

"Exactly!" Jae says. He moves to the front of the room. He is confident like a teacher right now. "It's not too late! We can still help the pandas. We can fix this. I remember the facts. Even without my script."

"We can put together a new presentation!" Whitney says, standing. "I remember how!"

"What about our habitat?" Chris asks. "It can't be fixed."

Gorkem responds, "We can turn it into something new!"

"Yeah," Brayden agrees.

"I'll help," I offer.

"Me too," Ella says. She walks to the front of the room to join Jae. "What if we set up the pieces from the habitat to decorate the lawn for the showcase? The whole thing will feel like a bamboo forest!"

"Yeah!" Brayden, Gorkem, and Chris say together.

Ella continues, "Then I can start the show with panda jokes. I'll make up new ones. Then, Jae and Whitney can give the presentation with all the panda facts." She looks at

Margo. "Will you help, Margo?"

We all look at her now.

She blinks slow like she's trying not to cry. Margo finally nods.

Then she pulls a crumpled bundle of paper out of her desk.

"My script!" Jae says, shocked.

"I'm . . . sorry," Margo blubbers.

Jae takes the script from her. "Well, this will make things easier. Thanks, Margo," he says.

"There's more . . . ," Margo whispers. "I . . . was the one to ruin the habitat. It was so cool. I couldn't stand it being better than our plan. So I investigated. I just wanted to see how you put it together. When I moved closer and touched it . . . it all toppled down."

We all gasp.

Chris walks up to Margo. He stops at her desk and says, "We all did bad stuff."

Jae adds, "But we can all still help the pandas. What's next for the plan, Ella?"

Ella continues, "Well, we'll have to end the show with Bessie's amazing magic trick. Right, Bessie?"

I pop up onto my chair.

"Teeny Houdini to the rescue!" I announce.

We all laugh.

Ms. Stoltz peeks into the classroom. She tells us time-out is over and we can go play now. But none of us do. We are huddled on the carpet. Margo and I work together to draw a new plan. We all take a part to get the showcase together for tomorrow.

Ms. Stoltz joins us. She says, "I am proud of each of you. You learned how to compromise. Everyone gave a little. And you all are working together now, too. Well done."

We all smile.

Then we get back to work. We spend the rest of the afternoon on our parts of the plan. We practice, practice, practice. And we all help to set up the lawn. Because our panda showcase is not about being the best. It is about saving the pandas. And that is what we're going to do!

The buses arrive, and it's time to go home.

Ms. Stoltz says, "We are ready for our panda showcase tomorrow!" She smiles so big her star earrings jingle.

I tug-tug-tug her sweater. When she leans down, I whisper one last idea I have to add to the show.

Ms. Stoltz gasps. She says, "Bessie, if you can pull that off, it would be spectacular."

Spectacular is a surprise so good that the

only thing the audience can say is *WOW*.

And if anyone knows how to wow a crowd, it's me.

I will help make the panda showcase spectacular!

10

The Giant Panda
Showcase

After Mom and Daddy get home from work, I tell them about my surprise idea.

Daddy makes a quick phone call to make sure our idea will work. And Gramma makes us a fast family dinner. We have hot dogs in homemade sweet buns. Yummy!

Then Daddy and I get going. Mom, Bailey, and Gramma stay home. Because Mom has to pay bills. Bailey has homework. And Gramma has to put her hair in curlers.

We arrive at the metro station. Daddy lets me scan the card like a big kid. Just like Bailey. We have to wait for the train that says "Red Line."

On the train ride, Daddy reads the newspaper. I stick my face against the window. Even though all I can see is black and black and more black zooming by. I ask, "Are we there yet? Are we there yet?" every two seconds.

Finally, Daddy says, "We're here!"

At the zoo entrance, Ms. Deer meets us at the gate. The zoo is closed. But Daddy talked to her on the phone. And she agreed to let us in after hours.

I cannot wait to see baby Xiao again!

Once we cross the Asia trail, Ms. Deer tells us what baby Xiao has been up to.

"He's tried two more new foods," she says, leading the way. "He didn't love bananas, but he didn't hate them. He liked applesauce, too. But not as much as his sweet potatoes."

She points to the hammock in the outdoor habitat. She continues, "That's where he likes to take a nap. Sometimes he falls asleep there and we have to carry him in. Good thing he's still pretty tiny. For now."

Daddy nods along as she speaks. I listen, too. But I also use my magician's eyes to try to find baby Xiao. When we get to the indoor viewing area, I spy baby Xiao!

My heart goes flip-flop to see him again!

I move as close as I can to him. Daddy stands behind me and rests his hands on my shoulders.

Baby Xiao is sleeping. His mommy sleeps on her back and squishes herself against the wall. Just like Baby Rabbit likes to do, too. Baby Xiao is snuggled under her chin. She is giant. And he is tiny. So his whole body is curled between her arm and chin. Their fur moves up and down at the same time when they breathe. Like music.

I think about the 1,864 pandas that are losing their homes. And then can't be with their mommies. It makes my heart feel like mushy potatoes.

I walk away from the enclosure so baby Xiao can sleep. Then I tug-tug-tug on the zookeeper's sleeve. When I have her attention, I tell her about our panda showcase. And how our class wants to help save the pandas. Then I ask her about my surprise idea.

The next evening, it is finally time for the panda showcase. Bailey helps make my hair look like panda bear ears. She also gave Gramma permission to fix her black-and-white ballet costume. It fits way better now. Baby Rabbit cannot come. She gives me a good-luck kiss and whisker twitch before I go.

Daddy wears my magician's hat for me since I sport my panda hairdo. Mom makes sure we arrive on time.

Our class greets everyone as others start to enter. Ella, Jae, Margo, Whitney, Brayden, Chris, Gorkem, and I all walk around and offer a juice box to each of our guests. We say, "Thank you for coming!"

There are lots and lots of people here! Ms. Wolff even dressed up like a bamboo tree to

show support. Ms. Pat, our bus driver, came, too. And she brought her sons, Trevon and Terry. Our neighbor, Ms. Alrahhal, walks right over to Gramma. She introduces more of her big family to us. Bailey invited all her friends and their families, too.

Our nice lunch lady, Ms. Alma, walks up to me. "I heard you did all this," she says. She points around us to the bamboo posts with twinkle lights strung all around them.

"Brayden, Chris, and Gorkem did most of the decorations. They used the stuff from their destroyed habitat. Margo and I added the twinkle lights. We all helped," I say.

"Neato!" she replies. Then she offers me a cookie from the giant cookie tray she is carrying! She says people will spend more money if their bellies are happy. She is so smart.

"Thank you for coming, Ms. Alma!" I say. I gobble up a warm chocolate chip cookie.

Finally, it is time to get started.

Ms. Stoltz gets everyone's attention with her bell.

Everyone takes a seat on the lawn chairs we set up.

Then she says, "Wow, what a turnout. Our first-grade class met some pandas earlier this week at the zoo. We learned how they are losing their homes. And how the zoo is doing so much to help them. Then our class decided we must help, too. This was all their idea. Their giant panda plan. Let's begin!"

Ella walks up in front of the large projector screen. She looks so great in the panda costume.

She clears her throat. Then begins her joke: "What is white, black, black, white, white, black, black, white?"

She pauses. Then answers, "A panda rolling down a hill!"

Everyone laughs and claps.

The rest of her jokes are a hit, too. Soon, the whole crowd is having fun.

Then Jae, Margo, and Whitney take turns presenting their slideshow. It is fancy! And full of panda facts.

"Why are pandas black-and-white?" Margo asks the audience.

"Camouflage," someone says.

"Panda!" a toddler shouts.

"Black to attract the sun, white to reflect it," Daddy calls out.

"You are all right. And you are all wrong," Whitney steps up and says.

Then Jae explains, "There are many

theories. But scientists are not really sure why pandas are black-and-white. Here is what they do know. . . ."

Everyone leans closer to the edge of their seat. Jae shows a photograph of baby Xiao. He shows all his research on why pandas are vulnerable. He talks about illegal hunting, deforestation, reproduction, and what pandas need to survive.

"We can stop cutting down the forests. We can use our voices to say STOP! And HELP! We can learn more. And we can donate to the zoo. They are helping pandas a lot," Jae declares. His voice is clear and loud. He stands sturdy like a strong tree.

Some people wipe tears from their faces. Because the presentation is very, very good.

Finally, it is time for me to perform my magic trick.

I walk in front of the projector screen. Whitney clicks the remote. Now the screen shows a stage. How perfect!

I address the audience, "Hello! I am Teeny Houdini. Tonight, I will perform the Big Bear Knot trick!" I reach into my magician's cape pocket and pull out the rope. "See how it is black-and-white like a panda bear?" I ask.

I hear Bailey giggle. Gramma claps.

"First, I need to make the rope magic." I hold my wand in one hand and the rope in the other. I tap the rope three times.

I drop my wand and wave my magical cape. "Now I will turn the rope into a panda bear." I move my hands fast like I practiced with Bailey. The rope has a large knot in the middle and two small loops on top of the big knot. It looks like a bear.

The audience *oohs*.

They are on the tippy edge of their seats.

They want to know what I will do next.

11

Ta-Da!

My audience watches me. I slowly walk around to show everyone the magic rope with a giant knot that looks like a panda bear.

"You see the bear?" I ask, returning in front of my screen-stage.

"Yes," someone in the audience responds.

"Now it will disappear! One, two, three. Abracadabra-poof!" I yell. I pull the rope tight. The bear knot vanishes.

"TA-DA!"

The crowd cheers. I take a bow. Then I stand back up, as tall as I can.

"There's more," I say. I sneaky-smile.

"Woo-hoo! Encore!" Bailey cheers from the crowd.

An *encore* is a surprise end after the end. And that's exactly what I am about to do.

"Just one moment, please." I announce. "This magician needs a minute to prepare!"

Everyone laughs. Mom says I was made for the stage.

I jump behind a row of bushes to get ready. No one knows what is behind this bush. Except me, Ms. Stoltz, and Daddy. Also, Ella and Jae. Because they are my magician's assistants tonight.

When I come back to the screen-stage, I am wearing blue zookeeper coveralls. And gloves. It is part of the surprise.

"Would you like to see the trick again?" I ask.

"Yeah!" the crowd cheers.

"Okay," I say. I hold the rope stretched tight with both hands.

Then I repeat my important message, "You saw the bear. You saw it disappear. Who will donate to our fundraiser? Who wants to see the bear again?"

Everyone laughs. But they all raise their hands, too.

I nod.

Ella walks over and unties my magic cape.

Then she and Jae throw it over my arms.

"One, two, three. Abracadabra-poof!" I say.

Jae pulls my magic cape away. Glitter flies everywhere.

The crowd is silent. Everyone's mouth hangs open. They. Are. Wowed.

Because in my arms, I do not carry the magic rope.

In my arms, I am cradling the real baby panda, Xiao!

Everyone stands and claps. There is whistling, too. And lots of cheering. This is called a standing ovation.

I smile so big my face hurts. But I cannot stop smiling.

I try to be very still so that I do not scare the baby panda.

Xiao looks up at me and chirps.

I lean down and whis-per to baby Xiao, "I will help you, baby Xiao, I promise."

Once I hand him back to the zookeeper, she lets the audience ask her questions. Then everyone opens their purses and wallets. Ms. Stoltz collects all their donations in a basket.

Mom runs over and gives me a big hug.

Later, Ms. Stoltz rings her bell again.

"I have an exciting announcement. Because of our first graders' superb showcase and our community's generous donations, we have raised one thousand dollars."

Everyone cheers.

Ms. Deer adds, "Thank you all so much. This amount will go toward sending a research team to China. Our team will find better ways to protect and care for the pandas. And it is all because of this class. Every little bit makes a big difference."

Families begin hugging. Gramma and Mom walk over to chat with Margo and her mom, who are wearing matching skirts. My

friends jump up and down. We high-five each
other.

Daddy hands me back my magician's hat.
I tug it over my panda ear
buns. Glitter falls
from the hat onto
my face.

I think about
what we did. A
teeny magician had
an idea. A little magic
show made real change for baby Xiao and the
giant pandas. And a class that cared brought
our whole community together.

Now, that . . . is BIG magic.

TA-DA!

The Real Baby Panda!

There is a real baby panda named Xiao Qi Ji at the Smithsonian National Zoo in Washington, DC. He was born August 21, 2020. He loves sweet potatoes and sleeping in the hammock. You can watch him on the zoo's Giant Panda Cam and learn more about him here:

nationalzoo.si.edu/animals/giant-panda

More Fun Facts:

+ Pandas can chirp, honk, bleat, chomp, and bark.

+ When Xiao Qi Ji was born, he weighed 4.9 ounces, only one thousandth of his mom's weight.

+ Male pandas will grow to weigh up to 250 pounds.

+ Each panda has a unique bite mark (just like each person's fingerprint).

+ Pandas can spend up to sixteen hours a day eating.

- Though they mostly eat bamboo, wild pandas sometimes eat birds, rodents, and fruit, too.

Help Save the Pandas!

Wild pandas live mainly in bamboo forests that are high in the mountains in China. There are sixty-seven protected panda reserves around there. That is where two thirds of all the wild pandas live. Thanks to protection efforts, the number of pandas is on the rise! But some subspecies remain in danger. And the natural habitat of pandas is still shrinking.

Pandas in the wild usually live fifteen to twenty years. But pandas living under human care, like at zoos, can live more than thirty years.

The Smithsonian's National Zoo and Conservation Biology Institute does a lot of work to protect and care for pandas. They work with scientists across the world and spend months in China every year to study wild pandas. They want to save all the pandas. You can help! Find out more here:

nationalzoo.si.edu/support/donate